TILLY'S PONY TAILS

Solo
the super star

PIPPA FUNNELL

Illustrated by Jennifer Miles

Orion
Children's Books

First published in Great Britain in 2010
by Orion Children's Books
a division of the Orion Publishing Group Ltd
Orion House
5 Upper St Martin's Lane
London WC2H 9EA
An Hachette UK Company

1 3 5 7 9 8 6 4 2

A catalogue record for this book is available from the British Library.

ISBN 978 1 84255 714 3

Printed and bound in the UK by CPI Mackays, Chatham ME5 8TD

www.orionbooks.co.uk
www.tillysponytails.co.uk

For my godson, Harry Wales

One

Tilly Redbrow was pleased that the summer was here. She didn't mind getting up early to go down to Silver Shoe Farm to feed and muck out the horses, but it was always easier when it was light outside and the weather was warm. She'd been helping out at the farm for almost a year now and had learned so much about looking after ponies and riding.

She loved every bit of it.

The thing she was most looking forward to, however, was her first ever Pony Club competition. Shows and rallies were being arranged throughout the holidays. Every weekend, horseboxes were being loaded up in the yard; and in the club room, people were constantly chatting about where they were taking their horses next. The atmosphere was great.

With only a few days to go before the Seaton Show, Tilly was keen to get as much practice in as possible. She would be jumping her strawberry roan, Rosie, in the smallest class, which was especially for

beginners. Tilly shared ownership of Rosie with her friend Mia. Mia would be jumping Rosie in the next, slightly bigger, class, so it was going to be a busy day for the little pony!

8

Angela, the owner of Silver Shoe Farm, was certain Tilly was ready for her first competition. After years of dreaming about being able to ride and compete, it was thrilling for Tilly to be able to do it for real. Angela had seen Tilly's skills and confidence improve enormously. She'd been giving her riding lessons ever since she'd joined Silver Shoe Farm after helping to rescue Magic Spirit, an abandoned horse, who had quickly become Tilly's favourite.

"Come on then, Tilly. Now you're warmed up, let's start popping over the cross pole," she called, pointing towards a single cross pole in the middle of the schooling area.

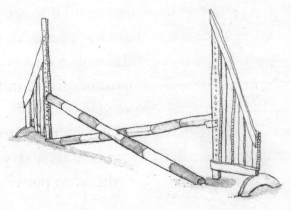

"Remember to interfere as little as possible. Keep your heels down, hands quiet, and see how still you can sit. I don't want to see any driving with your bottom," said Angela.

Tilly always found this difficult. Rosie could be on the lazy side, so Tilly had developed a habit of pushing with her seat, rather than using her legs, which Angela had quickly spotted.

"That's it," encouraged Angela. "You've got plenty of room, get nice and straight on your approach."

Tilly and Rosie moved directly towards the jump. Tilly made sure she was very calm in the last few strides, so as not to disturb Rosie's concentration. Then they took off together, and as Rosie popped over the cross pole, Tilly concentrated on looking straight ahead and riding away from the fence. Angela had explained to her before that the first landing stride after a jump was the first approach stride to the next fence.

"Make sure you follow enough with your arms over the top of the jump, and be careful not to thud into that saddle," warned Angela. "The impact of the landing needs to be absorbed through your knees and ankles."

Tilly repeated the simple exercise several times until she really found her rhythm.

"I'm impressed," said Angela. "Remember to keep your hands as still as possible. If you watch top show jumpers you'll see that their hands barely move. Do you think you're ready to try again? This time I'll add a small vertical four strides from the cross and you can jump both of them."

Tilly drew a deep breath and nudged Rosie back into a canter towards the jumps. She knew that practice was important – no time to waste. She also knew there was no room for negativity. Duncan, who was Angela's head boy and a talented rider, always said that riders needed to 'commit' to the jump; once they'd started there

should be no indecision, just positive
forward thinking.

But negative thoughts were never a
problem for Tilly. Even when she was
nervous about something, she was
determined to conquer her fears and go for it.

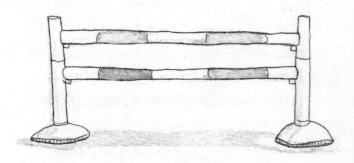

Following Angela and Duncan's advice,
she took a moment to think about how she
could improve the approach, and then
advanced towards the first cross pole. She
was rewarded when Rosie sailed over it
very neatly. There was just enough time for
Tilly to regain her balance and for Rosie to
adjust her canter, before they were up and
jumping the vertical. Perfect!

"Thank you, girl," said Tilly, patting Rosie's neck. As brave as Tilly had been, she realised that most of the effort had been Rosie's. Nevertheless, Tilly did feel quietly excited about the forthcoming competition – she just hoped they could jump as well as they had done today.

After her lesson, Tilly went to the stables to see the other important horse in her life – Magic Spirit. Tilly and Magic had been through a lot together. She had been the only person he'd felt confident around when he first arrived at the stables. She'd groomed and cared for him. She'd helped Duncan break him in, and seen him grow from an unpredictable, nervous animal into a calm and cooperative ride. When Magic had had colic, she'd stayed by his side and helped nurse him back to health. They were best friends.

As she entered the stall, Tilly adjusted

the horsehair bracelet her mum had made her. It contained hairs from Magic's tail and matched the other one she had worn all her life. When she was little she'd had to loop this bracelet round her wrist several times, but as she grew it fitted better. Tilly had never known her real mum and dad. Her mum had died just after she was born, and for as long as she could remember, Tilly had happily been a member of the Redbrow family.

The only link Tilly had to her past was an old photograph and the bracelet. There was something special about it – it was like a lucky talisman. Tilly never took it off.

"Hello, boy!" she said, as Magic came towards her. He fussed over her, sniffing her hair and nuzzling her cheeks. It didn't

matter that he couldn't say how much he adored Tilly – it was obvious from the way he reacted.

Tilly produced a fresh carrot from her pocket, which he munched eagerly, while she stroked his neck. They were alone together for several minutes, until Duncan appeared, lugging a bucket of water.

"Hi, Tilly. How's Magic?"

"He's in a chirpy mood. He likes the sun."

"We'll turn him out in a minute – so he can graze in the long field with the others. I've been thinking, Tilly . . ."

Duncan sounded as though he was going to say something interesting.

"I've got a few hours spare tomorrow morning. Maybe it's time I got you in the saddle. Time for your first ride on Magic Spirit."

Tilly gasped. She had wanted to ride Magic since she'd first set eyes on him. Duncan hadn't wanted to rush into it though, because he had to make sure it was totally safe.

"I believe he's ready. He's had enough experience with Jack Fisher and me now. And *you're* definitely ready – Angela tells me you're doing great with your lessons."

Tilly grinned and blushed.

"Let's meet here tomorrow morning then. About ten o'clock. Is that okay with you?"

"Yeah!" said Tilly, eyes wide with excitement.

"And is it also okay with *you*?" Duncan smiled at Magic. Magic lifted his head and shook it gleefully.

"That's a yes, then!"

Two

Tilly was so thrilled about the thought of riding Magic Spirit, she couldn't eat her breakfast.

"You'll need the energy," her mum protested. "It's a big weekend for you. Competition day tomorrow."

Reluctantly, Tilly forced down half a bowl of muesli, then she was up and away from the table. She needed time to

polish her jodhpur boots and plait her hair –
it always took ages because it was so long.

Half an hour later, she and her dad were
driving through the tunnel of silver birches
which led to Silver Shoe Farm. It was Tilly's
number one favourite journey, and today it
looked particularly lovely, as sunlight filtered
through the fresh young leaves.

Mr Redbrow pulled the car into the
lane and Tilly hopped out.

"See you later, Dad."

"Bye, Tiger Lil'. Have a good ride. And
make sure Magic behaves himself."

Tilly could detect a hint of worry in his
voice. He was concerned about Magic
being so much bigger than Rosie, but she
knew he wouldn't interfere. When there
was something Tilly wanted, especially
when it came to horses, nothing would
stand in her way.

Duncan was waiting for her at the five-
bar gate. He was holding a black leather
saddle over his arm. The sight of it made
her shiver with excitement.

"He's as keen as you are," said Duncan, smiling. "Let's get him groomed and ready."

Tilly followed Duncan. She stopped off at the tack room to get her grooming kit, and then went to greet Magic. He was standing in the yard, swishing his tail. Duncan had already tied him up, so Tilly started brushing his coat. He was clean already, but she wanted to make sure there were no specks of dirt that might rub – everything about this ride was going to be perfect.

After a good groom with a body brush
and curry comb, Tilly neatened his mane
by dampening it down with a wet brush
and then combed his tail. She sponged his
eyes, nostrils and dock and, seeing that
Duncan had already picked out his hooves,
she put some hoof oil on them. She
remembered how, when she'd first started
grooming him, it had taken her ages. She
was much quicker, and more efficient, now
that she'd had lots of practice. She finished
the process by kissing him on the nose.

"You look beautiful, Magic," she whispered. "The best horse in the whole world."

Duncan helped Tilly to tack up, making sure every strap and buckle was securely fitted, then they led Magic down to the schooling area. A lesson had just finished so they had the whole space to themselves.

"I've brought this to help," said Duncan, as he placed a wooden step by Magic's side. "At 16hh, you'll certainly notice the difference between him and Rosie. This will make it easier for you to climb on."

Magic stood very still, but as Tilly looked at the wooden step and then up at the height of his back, she started to see what her dad had been worrying about. Magic seemed huge! She tugged anxiously on her horsehair bracelets and contemplated how to go about mounting.

"Don't worry if it's a bit scary," said Duncan reassuringly. "The difference between a pony and a horse is bound to be a shock. You'll get used to it though. Soon enough, you'll grow out of Rosie and you'll *have* to ride a horse."

Tilly nodded and took a deep, strengthening breath. She gripped Magic's withers, stepped on to the wooden block, slipped her left foot into the stirrup iron and then swung her right leg up and over. No problem.

Duncan leaned forward and tightened the girth. Tilly glanced at the ground and realised how high up she was. Everything seemed a long way away, but she didn't panic. She knew she was in safe hands with Magic and Duncan. And besides, this was it – the moment she'd been waiting for.

"All set," said Duncan, patting Magic's shoulder. "I'll lead you for a few circuits, Tilly, then you can go on your own. Give you a chance to see how well we've trained him. He's very responsive."

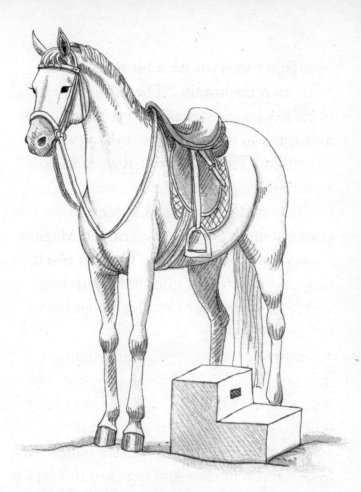

They walked around the arena twice
and Tilly couldn't believe how comfortable
Magic felt, and how naturally she found her
balance – especially considering the extra
length of Magic's stride. It was clear he was
destined to become a super star.

After several more laps, Duncan unclipped the lead rope.

"Off you go," he said. "You're on your own now."

And off Tilly went, turning left and right, circling, and changing pace. Magic did everything she asked, and as far as Tilly was concerned, he did it more fluidly than any

horse in the world. He was amazing! Magic was her first top class ride, and he definitely lived up to his name – he *felt* like magic!

As they worked round the arena, Tilly imagined crowds of people watching in awe:

"There go the champions! Tiger Lily and Magic Spirit! Apparently they're inseparable. They only work for each other!"

She didn't want the ride to end, but
Duncan assured her there'd be other
chances.

Eventually, Tilly drew to a halt and,
after patting Magic's neck and showering
him with compliments, she dismounted
and went over to Duncan.

"You looked great on him," he said.
"Angela will be so pleased – she said he'd
be right for you. Hopefully you'll have a
good future together, when you've grown
a few inches, that is."

These last comments made Tilly blink
and wonder.

What did he mean by that? Was he
hinting that Angela had plans for Magic
and her? The idea was mind-boggling and
far too exciting to dare thinking about for
long!

Three

That evening, around the dinner table, Tilly couldn't stop talking about her ride on Magic Spirit. She prodded at a plate of homemade chilli, and several times, her mum had to remind her to eat rather than talk. But when she wasn't talking about the ride, she was thinking about it. Thankfully it was a good distraction from getting nervous about the next day's competition.

"Early night for you, Tilly," said her dad. "You want to be fresh for tomorrow."

Tilly didn't mind. She'd read lots of articles about competing and knew it was important to get plenty of rest beforehand. She helped with the dishes then went straight up to her room.

She didn't go to sleep though. There was too much stuff whirring around her head.

Tilly went to the little box on her dressing table and opened it. Inside was the tattered photograph of her birth mum – the one that her adoptive mum had given to her, the day before her first Pony Club camp. She sat on the edge of her bed, resting her feet on a pile of old *Pony* magazines, and stared at it. Her mum, who looked just like her, was dressed in a Native American costume, hands resting on her tummy, standing next to a beautiful Appaloosa horse.

"I wish I knew more about you," she whispered. "And who that lovely horse is."

Suddenly, she wanted more than anything to be able to tell this familiar woman in the photograph all about her

adventures with Magic Spirit. She wanted
so much to tell her about the ride, about
the competition tomorrow, and about how
well she was doing with her jumping. She
wanted to talk about her friends at Silver
Shoe Farm, how she shared Rosie with
Mia, and how together, they'd watched the

birth of the farm's new foal, Lucky Chance.

"Maybe one day, one day, I'll find out who you were," she sighed, then placed the photograph back in the box.

Tilly checked her clothes for the next day. She'd made a list of things that she needed: a clean shirt, jodhpurs, gloves, hat, and of course, her Pony Club tie. She folded them neatly and pinned her Pony Club badge to the tweed riding jacket that one of the girls at Silver Shoe had lent her. The afternoon before, she had polished her boots and cleaned her tack, so it was all ready and waiting for her at Silver Shoe Farm. They were leaving early, taking Rosie by horsebox.

clean shirt
jodhpurs
gloves
hat
pony club tie

Finally everything was ready. Time for sleep.

32

It wasn't until Tilly arrived at the stables next morning that she started to think clearly. It was a gorgeous day, blue skies and a warm breeze. Mia was in the yard, checking Rosie over and making sure she was fit to travel.

"Hi, Tilly. I've fed and groomed her already. Will you do her plaits? You're so much better at them than me!"

"Sure," said Tilly. She loved plaiting Rosie's mane. She was able to get it really neat – thanks to all that practice on her own hair!

Standing on a small wooden box, Tilly started dividing Rosie's mane into equal-sized bunches. Tilly knew from the books she'd read that you could secure horses' plaits with either bands or special plaiting thread – she'd opted for the thread today, so Rosie's plaits would be neater and more secure.

One by one, Tilly plaited twelve little bunches, rolled them up, then sewed them into place with a special plaiting needle

and thread. When she'd finished Rosie's
neck, Mia held Rosie's head, while Tilly
plaited her forelock.

"You've done a beautiful job!"
exclaimed Mia. "She'll be the smartest
pony at the show."

Finally, Tilly added Rosie's tail
bandage, and Mia put on some travelling
boots and a smart blue-chequered
competition rug.

Now Rosie was dressed, it was time to load her into the box. Mia took the lead rope and walked her straight up the ramp, while Tilly made sure the breeching strap was in place. They checked she was content and comfortable and then stood to the side and raised the ramp.

"All set?" said Mia's mum. "Do you want to just double check all the tack and equipment is in?

"Oh!" said Tilly, suddenly remembering. "I'd almost forgotten the hay-net and water – thanks!"

Mia's mum was driving them to the show. It was lucky she owned a powerful four-wheel drive – ideal for towing trailers. When they were all packed, she walked round the vehicle and checked everything was ready.

"Let's get going then. We don't want to be late, and the car park is bound to be busy!"

Mia and Tilly jumped into the back and put their seatbelts on. Just as they were

about to leave, Angela came out of the club room, clutching a mug of coffee. She waved them off and called out,

"Good luck and enjoy yourselves!"

They waved back eagerly, and as the car turned out of the gate, Mia and Tilly looked at each other.

"I've got a feeling this is going to be the start of great day," said Tilly, smiling happily.

"High five!" said Mia, holding up her left hand. Tilly smacked it, and they both fell about laughing.

Four

As Mia's mum had warned, the car park
was crowded with horseboxes and trailers.
For her it was stressful, trying to find
somewhere to park and safely unload
Rosie. But for Tilly and Mia it was all very
thrilling. There were people and horses
everywhere!

"Look! There's Cally and Mr Fudge!"
said Mia, tapping on the window.

Cally was their good friend. She and
Mia used to share Rosie, before Cally

moved to Cavendish Hall, the exclusive boarding school in North Cosford, and got a pony of her own, Mr Fudge.

As soon as Cally saw the girls, she waved frantically, but she couldn't come over, because Mr Fudge was getting impatient with all the hustle and bustle of the car park.

"I'll text you!" she mouthed, pointing to the pocket where she kept her mobile.

At last, Mia's mum found a big space to park in, with plenty of shade and room to get Rosie out.

"Right then. Let's unload."

"I hope she's had a good journey," said Tilly.

"She's usually a good traveller," said Mia. "Once we took her all the way to Leeds!"

Tilly climbed into the box and greeted Rosie, who was standing perfectly calmly. She untied her, as Mia released the ramp and breeching strap.

"You'll need to back her out as straight and steadily as you can," called Mia.

Together, the girls manoeuvred Rosie out of the trailer. Tilly concentrated hard because she didn't want to make a mistake and upset the little pony. Once Rosie was out, they tacked her up ready for the first class. She was more fidgety than usual, and Tilly guessed she must be excited to be at a party. They did what they could to settle her, but there was too much distraction.

"It's much easier when the venue is close by and we can hack to it," moaned Mia. "Hopefully the next one will be local."

"Need a hand?" came a familiar voice behind them.

Tilly turned and smiled. It was Brook Ashton-Smith, from Cavendish Hall. Tilly had met him a few times, and used her whispering skills to help him with his beautiful black horse, Solo. Mia started to blush, because she thought Brook was good-looking.

"Hi, Brook," said Tilly. "Are you competing today?"

"Er, yeah. I hope I am," Brook replied, although he sounded a bit agitated. "Is Rosie being tricky? Let me help you hold her."

He came towards them, and stood on the opposite side, holding Rosie. With him present, Rosie suddenly calmed.

"She obviously likes you," grinned Tilly.

Brook didn't reply and Tilly could tell that there was something bothering him.

"Are you nervous about your competition?" she asked.

"Don't ask things like that," said Mia. "Brook doesn't have *anything* to be nervous about!"

But Tilly knew otherwise. She felt as if she could say anything to Brook and he wouldn't mind.

"Um, I am a bit actually," said Brook, looking glum. "You see, I've lost my lucky talisman. I've had it all my life and I never compete without it. I can't find it and now I'm really worried."

"That's awful," said Tilly, imagining how much she'd hate it if she lost one of her horsehair bracelets. They were precious to her – the one she was adopted with, and the one her mum had made her. In fact they were *so* special to her that she'd started making them for her friends too. One for Duncan, from Red Admiral's tail, which she'd given him after he and Red

42

won the Cosford Derby; one from Rosie's tail for her friend Cally; and one for Jean-Paul, the jockey who'd won the Puissance at Olympia on his stallion, Samson. She sensed these bracelets were just as special to her friends as they were to her.

"Yeah, I don't know what happened. I thought I had it when I got changed and when I went back to my kit bag, it had *gone*! Maybe I dropped it somewhere," he said, scratching his head.

"Try not to worry," said Tilly hopefully. "I'm sure it will turn up."

But Tilly knew that was easier said than done. Brook wasn't himself at all, so the talisman obviously meant a lot to him.

A while later, Tilly and Mia were waiting with Rosie, watching some of the youngest Pony Club members parading their tiny ponies.

"They're so cute!" gushed Mia.

"Where are the toilets?" said Tilly. "I should go before my competition."

"Good idea. They're in the changing block, beside the judges' shelter. Go now or you might be too late."

Tilly rushed through the crowds and found the block. There were rows of low wooden benches, piled with people's kit bags. Everything smelled of bleach and hairspray. A group of girls in riding jackets were fussing round a mirror, trying to get their hair into nets. They were giggling loudly.

Tilly shuffled past them and into one of the cubicles. She couldn't help overhearing their conversation – they were being so loud.

"Have you got it!" shrieked one of them.

"*Yes!* Check this out!"

"Where did you find it?"

"It was lying on top of his bag. He says it's lucky."

"Let me touch it!"

"No! Me first, I found it!"

There were lots of voices all at once, giggles and gasps. Tilly could hardly believe her ears.

"We should put it back though. We can't steal it."

"We aren't going to *steal* it. We're just looking at it!"

"He's so gorgeous. Do you think if I hold it for long enough he'll fall in love with me?!"

Tilly's mouth dropped open. She sat in silence, hoping the girls would forget she

was there. She knew what they were up to. They were obviously members of some kind of Brook Ashton-Smith fan club, and had taken his lucky talisman when he wasn't looking. How silly – they probably had no idea of the upset they had caused.

Five

Tilly waited in the cubicle, anxiously checking her watch, until the girls left. The last thing she heard them say was, "Put it back now. Come on, let's go!"

She hoped she might be able to find the lucky talisman and return it to Brook before he competed, but as she crept into the empty changing room, feeling a bit like a private detective, she realised how difficult it would be. There were hundreds of kit bags, of all different shapes, colours

and sizes. She had no idea which one belonged to Brook and it was a race against the clock if she was going to get to her own class on time.

She began checking the bags for name labels, but it was no use. It would take too long. She needed to find Brook and tell him what had happened, then he could come and get the talisman himself.

"There you are!" cried Mia, as Tilly stepped into the sunlight. "Your name's been called – it's the first class and you're up. You've got to get Rosie to the competition ring right away. I'll take you there. Come on."

"But . . ." said Tilly.

It was clear that Mia meant business. There was no time to waste, and the last thing Tilly wanted was to miss her own competition. Brook's lucky talisman would have to wait.

Tilly took Rosie's lead rope and, together, the girls marched towards the competition area. In some ways, Tilly was glad of the distractions in the changing rooms, because it had made her less nervous about what she was about to do.

"Come on, Rosie, girl. Be good for me, won't you?" she said encouragingly, patting Rosie on the shoulder. Rosie pricked her ears.

"Smile and say good morning," Mia suddenly whispered, nudging Tilly in the ribs.

"Why? Who to?" said Tilly, confused.

"Them."

Mia pointed to a group of very important-looking people, dressed in dark suits and bowler hats.

"They're the officials. They'll be judging your competition. It always pays to be polite."

As the girls walked past, they nodded and smiled. The officials smiled back, as Rosie stopped walking and began to lift her tail.

"Uh oh," groaned Mia.

Sure enough, Rosie stood still and did her business. There was nothing that Tilly or Mia could do. They waited beside her, with fixed grins on their faces, while the officials continued smiling back.

Finally, it was time to move on again.

"How embarrassing," said Mia.

"When she's got to go, she's got to go!" said Tilly, giggling. "I guess the officials are used to it."

Mia's mum held Rosie beside the collecting ring while Mia and Tilly walked around the ten-fence show jumping course. Trying to remember all she'd been taught, Tilly studied the course carefully.

"You'll be fine, Tilly. Just make sure you don't cut the corners and try to make use of the whole ring," said Mia. "Good luck!"

Then she gave Tilly a quick hug, and went to find a place where she'd get a good view of the action.

Tilly took a deep breath. From now on she was on her own. She checked her clothes; she'd polished her riding boots so much she could see her own reflection in them. She was wearing her favourite cream jodhpurs, with a white shirt, and a tweed jacket. Her plaits were neatly tucked under her crash helmet and her Pony Club badge was pinned in place.

Rosie was looking good too. Mia had groomed her thoroughly and her coat was gleaming. Her tack was clean, and her plaits, thanks to Tilly, were some of the neatest on show.

"Ready then, Rosie?" she whispered.

Just a few moments to twist her
horsehair bracelets and think of good things
– like the photograph of her real mum, her

lovely family, her
first ride on Magic
Spirit, and all the
wonderful horses in
the world. Then it
was time to get on,
warm up over
a few small jumps,
and wait for her
turn.

Tilly was second
to go, so she had the
chance to watch the
girl who went before
her. The girl's pony was lovely – a pretty
chestnut with white socks, slightly smaller
than Rosie. Their jumping was a bit wobbly.
They seemed to approach each one at a
wonky angle, and Tilly could tell the girl
was over-checking, fussing too much before
the jump – maybe it was nerves.

She knew she had to avoid those things, and remember everything that Angela and Duncan had taught her.

Finally she heard her name announced over the loudspeaker:

"Miss Tiger Lily Redbrow, from Silver Shoe Farm, riding Rosebud."

The adrenalin took over.

Tilly straightened up and sat taller as she asked Rosie to walk on. As soon as they were inside the ring, she could feel all eyes upon her. It was truly nerve-wracking, but she and Rosie had practised and practised. They only had to do the things they'd prepared for. They didn't have to worry about anyone else.

The jumps were well spaced and Tilly realised she'd have plenty of time to allow Rosie to find her stride pattern before each one. It made her feel confident.

Six

Tilly cantered Rosie around the ring, came back to a walk, then saluted the judges.

The bell rang.

She could feel the butterflies in her tummy, but as soon as Rosie started to canter again, Tilly's nerves went away as she focused all her energy on the task ahead.

Rhythm and balance. Keep it smooth. She could hear Angela's words in her head.

One by one, Rosie tackled the jumps, and Tilly thought it felt almost effortless.

Everything seemed to be going really well until they came to the second to last jump, which was a double. Tilly missed her stride but managed to stay in balance. She gave the rein as much as she could, being careful not to catch Rosie in the mouth with her hands. Then, thanks to quick thinking and extra effort on Rosie's part, Tilly recovered enough to jump the last fence.

"Clear round," announced the commentator.

Tilly's huge smile said it all. Rosie's neck must have been numb from the amount of patting she received! Imagine this feeling amplified a million times, Tilly thought to herself. That's what it would feel like to compete in a major event like Badminton or Burghley, or even the

Olympics. One day. Maybe.

She and Rosie walked out of the ring, passing the girl who was going to jump next.

"Good luck!" Tilly said, smiling.

The girl smiled back, but she looked worried.

Mia met them at the edge of the collecting ring and held Rosie as Tilly dismounted.

"You were great!" she cheered. "The best – high five for Silver Shoe Farm!"

"High five!" Tilly agreed, clapping and shaking Mia's hand.

They led Rosie away from the crowds
and then went to find out Tilly's score. The
class Tilly had just done was a special one –
penalties were given for jumping, but
points were also awarded for style. This
was awarded by a different judge, and it
helped encourage competitors to think
about improving their riding skills.

As Tilly and Mia waited at the
secretaries' tent, which was busy with
riders all wanting the same information,
they felt someone jump up behind them.
It was Cally.

"Hi, guys! I've been looking for you
everywhere. I just saw you jump, Tilly –
you've got the knack of it so quickly!
What's your secret?"

Tilly thought about what Angela might
say.

"Hard work, dedication and practice,"
she nodded.

"You sound like Angela," said Mia,
rolling her eyes.

Tilly shrugged.

"Who else is here from Cavendish Hall?"

"Lots of people," said Cally. "Sabrina and Jessica – remember them from Pony Club camp? They're competing this afternoon. There are a few girls from the years above me, and some of the sixth formers – Brook's here."

Tilly suddenly remembered what had happened with the lucky talisman.

"Do you know where he is?" she asked.

"I saw him a few minutes ago. He's at the entrance to the main arena, pacing up and down. I think he's about to compete but he looks really dodgy . . ."

"I've got to find him. Meet me later, will you? I've got to go!"

"But . . .?" said Cally, confused.

"What about your score?" said Mia.

Too late. Tilly was already backing away from the secretaries' tent and weaving her way through the crowds. The score could wait. Although it was important to her, something inside made her feel sure that Brook mattered more.

She found him standing by the warm-up ring, chewing his fingernail. Solo was at his side, looking very shiny and well turned-out.

"Brook!" Tilly waved, trying to get his attention.

He turned and gave a worried smile.

"I think I know where it is," she called. "I think I can get you your lucky talisman back."

Brook's eyes widened.

"*Really?* How? Where?"

Then he looked at his watch. He shook his head.

"There's hardly any time. I'm competing in a minute."

"Leave it to me," said Tilly. "Just tell me what your kit bag looks like."

"It's green. It's got the Cavendish Hall logo on it, but you'll know it, because it's covered in biro and graffiti!"

"Right."

With that, Tilly raced towards the changing block. She burst through the door, nearly tripping on a pile of muddy riding boots, then began sifting through the bags. There were more than a dozen green Cavendish Hall ones. She picked up each one, examining them for biro and graffiti, then pushed them aside if they weren't right. No luck.

"Where *is* it?" she wondered, clamping her hands to her head. She stood very still and scanned the entire room. Finally, she spied one last green bag sticking out from beneath a group of pink, girly backpacks.

Straightaway, she knew it was the one. She tugged it free, and sure enough, it was covered in scrawled messages and cartoons.

The zip was undone, so she rummaged in the bag, searching for something that looked like a lucky talisman. There were spare socks, a clean white t-shirt, jodhpurs, boot polish, an iPod, a couple of bottles of water and a mushy banana. But no lucky talisman.

Once she'd removed everything, she straightened it out and placed it back in the bag. Suddenly her fingers caught on something. She pulled it, and realised it was her horsehair bracelet – the one her real mum had made for her when she was born. It must have slipped off her wrist as she was rummaging. The thought of nearly losing it made her heart skip a beat.

Immediately, she went to slip it back on her wrist. And as she did so, she realised her bracelet was already there. It hadn't slipped off at all. The one she was holding in her other hand, that she'd found in the bag, wasn't hers.

Brook's lucky talisman. It was a horsehair bracelet, identical to the one she

wore. A shiver passed through her – a weird feeling, as if something extraordinary was happening. But there was no time to lose. She had to get the bracelet back to Brook before he competed. She pivoted on the heels of her jodhpur boots, and in a flurry of amazement and curiosity, was gone again.

Seven

Brook was sitting on Solo, waiting anxiously in the collecting ring of the main arena. Tilly could see him, but a crowd of spectators and officials was making it difficult for her to get close. It was the main competition of the day, so it had attracted lots of people, including journalists and photographers from the Seaton Gazette.

"Excuse me! Excuse me!" Tilly said, trying to sound polite as she pushed her way through.

People seemed to be ignoring her and it was very frustrating. Without his lucky talisman, Brook wouldn't feel confident competing, and with all these people watching him – it was too much pressure! What if he did really badly, or worse, fell off!

A voice came over the loudspeaker:

"And now, in the senior show jumping group, competing for the prestigious Hoffman Cup, all the way from Cavendish Hall, we have Brook Ashton-Smith on Solo!"

The crowd cheered and Tilly noticed a group of girls jumping up and down and shrieking louder than everyone else. They were the ones who had hidden the bracelet. It will be *their* fault if things go wrong for Brook, thought Tilly crossly.

At last, she reached the edge of the collecting ring. Brook and Solo were just in front of her. Solo was twitching and shaking his head, as though he was itching to get going. Brook looked uneasy – it was only a matter of seconds before the clock started.

"I've got it! Brook! I've got it here!" Tilly cried. She waved the bracelet frantically.

"Sssh!" said a sharp voice beside her. "Don't distract him. He's about to compete."

Determined, Tilly shouted again.

"Brook! Over here!"

He turned and caught her eye. When he saw what was in her hand, a huge smile swept across his face. His shoulders sagged with relief and, nudging Solo with his leg, he came towards Tilly.

"Oh, Tilly! Thank you so much!

This means the world to me," he said, reaching down for the bracelet.

"It's strange, you know," said Tilly quietly, helping to tie it around his wrist. "But I've got one exactly the same. My real mum gave it to me when I was a baby, before I was adopted."

"You were . . . ? You were adopted? Show it to me."

Tilly lifted the cuff of her white shirt, revealing her own horsehair bracelet.

"It *is* the same!" exclaimed Brook. "When? *Where* were you adopted then?"

"I was looked after by a children's home. The Redbrow family adopted me after my mum died. I didn't have any other family."

Suddenly, the colour seemed to drain from Brook's face. He went very pale and quiet, as though he didn't know what to do or say next. Tilly stared up at him, wondering what he was thinking. Eventually he reached down, took one of her hands, and looked into her eyes.

"It's you," he whispered. "It's you."

"What do you mean?"

"*Brook!*"

Another voice interrupted them.

"*Brook!* Pay attention. You've been called twice. It's your turn. Get going."

There was no more time. Brook and Tilly's hands parted. With a powerful, eager pull, Solo veered away from the crowds and marched into the arena, leaving Tilly standing alone in bewilderment. What was all that about? What did Brook mean?

All she could do now was watch, hoping the last minute return of the lucky bracelet would make a difference. There were several different jumps set up in the arena.

71

Some looked enormous, and made the class she'd jumped seem tiny.

The first obstacle was an upright. Brook and Solo looked totally focused and unruffled as they approached it. Solo was beautiful to watch. His rhythm and balance were effortless. He hopped over the high gate as though it was nothing. He reminded Tilly of the amazing horses she had seen at the Olympia Horse Show.

The following obstacles were a parallel, and then a wall five strides later. They looked daunting, but Tilly knew Brook would cope. He was so professional in the way he tackled them. She could see why everyone talked about what a great horseman he would become one day. He barely seemed to move; he was completely relaxed and he kept his lower leg completely still.

Finally, they came to the combination. It was a triple, involving a parallel, an upright and another parallel. Tilly had seen combinations like this on television and

always thought they
looked difficult.
As Brook and
Solo made the
approach,
she held
her breath,
grabbed hold
of her horsehair
bracelet and
sent him good
thoughts.

She pictured the
photograph of her real mum
and the mysterious horse she was with.
Then, in her mind, the photograph came to
life. Her mum and the horse were galloping
across a prairie. Tilly imagined herself riding
alongside them on Magic Spirit. The wind
blew through their hair and the sky stretched
out above them. Suddenly, in this daydream,
Brook appeared. He and Solo caught up with
them, and like a little gang, they galloped
together. It felt wonderful.

A ripple of applause startled Tilly back
to reality. She realised she'd been miles
away and hadn't noticed the detail of
Brook's attempt at the combination. By the
sound of the crowd, he'd done well. The
group of annoying girls from the changing
rooms were waving Cavendish Hall hats
and chanting his name. Lucky for them,
thought Tilly, that she'd managed to get his
bracelet back to him.

Brook rode into the collecting ring and
dismounted. He looked
flushed but happy.
He signalled to
Tilly, pointing at
his mouth, as if
he was saying
he wanted to
talk more, but
before she
could get close
to him, he and
Solo were whisked
away by a group of

staff and pupils wearing Cavendish Hall
colours.

Eight

"There you are!" said Cally, with a mumsy tone to her voice.

"You keep disappearing," added Mia. "We've spent most of our day chasing after you! We've got the results of your show jumping competition."

Tilly had been so caught up in finding Brook's bracelet, she had almost forgotten about her own jumping. She felt a twinge of anticipation return.

"What? What is it? How did I do?"

"Well . . ." said Mia, lingering teasingly over her answer. "You got 8.4 points out of 10 for your style. Which means you came second – out of twenty other competitors!"

Tilly's jaw dropped open. She knew she'd jumped well, but not that well.

"Congrats, Tilly!" said Cally, giving her a hug. "That's such a good result. I think I came last in my first competition."

"And the girl who beat you, she got 9.2 points – not even a whole point ahead of you!"

Tilly was thrilled.

"Where's Rosie? I want to say well done to her."

"She's back at the trailer with Mr Fudge. Our mums are watching them. They've got some hay and have been offered water."

Tilly said she was going to check on her and meet up with the girls again later. Mia and Cally went off to get hot-dogs from the cafe.

"We'll get you one," said Cally.

Tilly made her way through the field. As she went, she texted her mum and dad, and then Angela and Duncan:

ME N ROSIE CAME SECOND! HAVING A GR8 TIME! XXX

Seconds later, her phone was bombarded with replies:

79

WELL DONE TIGER LIL! YOU'VE WORKED HARD AND DESERVE YOUR
SUCCESS. WE'LL CELEBRATE WHEN YOU GET HOME. LOVE DAD. X

GOOD STUFF TILLY. THE SILVER SHOE GANG ARE VERY PROUD
OF YOU. LOVE ANGELA. XX

I'M IN THE LONG FIELD WITH MAGIC. JUST TOLD HIM
YOUR NEWS. HE'S NODDING HIS HEAD – I THINK HE'S
IMPRESSED. WELL DONE. DUNCAN.

And then, moments after that:

MUM CAN'T WORK HER FONE. SHE TOLD ME 2 TXT U
ABOUT SOME HORSE THING. APPARENTLY U CAME
SECOND. WHY DIDN'T U COME FIRST, LOSER?
LOVE FROM UR PERFECT BROTHER ADAM. X

Tilly laughed.

Rosie was with her friends, standing
beneath the shade of an oak tree. It was
lovely to see them together. They were
hanging out just like their human owners did.

"Hello, gorgeous girl!" she said gently,
placing her arms around Rosie's neck. "Did

you hear we came second – thank you so much for being a wonderful, lovely pony!"

Rosie nuzzled Tilly's shoulder and sniffed at her plaits.

"I've brought you a treat."

Tilly held out a handful of Rosie's favourite mints. Within seconds they were gobbled up.

"Now, I think I'd better go and find Brook. He said he wanted to talk to me. I'll see you later."

Tilly stepped away, but Rosie followed after her, straining on her rope.

"Want to come with me, do you?"

Rosie snorted.

Tilly glanced at Mia's mum, who had been watching the ponies. She nodded in agreement, so Tilly undid Rosie's tie and led her away from the car park.

"Goodness knows how we're going to find him though, Rosie. There must be hundreds of people here," said Tilly, forgetting all about the hot-dog Cally and Mia were getting for her. "And lots of them

are wearing the Cavendish Hall colours.
He'll be difficult to spot."

Tilly and Rosie wandered from ring to ring
for twenty minutes, through the crowds,
past the main arena, the refreshment tent,
and the changing block. Back to the small
arena, where earlier, she and Rosie had had
their triumph (the sight of it made her
tingle with happiness!). Rosie was very
obedient and enjoyed being paraded about.
They saw lots of people but Brook was
nowhere to be found.

Eventually they came to a stop.

"This is impossible," Tilly sighed.

Rosie swished her tail, sharing Tilly's
frustration.

They stood and contemplated what to
do next. Suddenly, Rosie started stamping
her forefoot and nudging her head in the
direction of the secretaries' tent.

"What are you fussing for?" asked Tilly.

She realised that Rosie was interested in a group of horses gathered nearby. They were all wearing green anti-sweat rugs – the Cavendish Hall colour. And they were being tended by several Cavendish Hall staff. The biggest of the horses stepped to the side.

"It's Solo!" Tilly exclaimed.

"Of course! Wherever Solo is, Brook will be close behind. Well done, Rosie! Good idea. We'll wait here until Brook shows up."

She approached one of the staff, who was sponging down the neck of a large bay.

"Excuse me, do you know where Brook Ashton-Smith is?"

"He's collecting his trophy. He came first in the Seniors' group. He'll be along in a minute."

Tilly beamed. She was so happy for Brook. Coming first, especially after the stress of losing his bracelet . . . the horsehair bracelet, that's what he wanted to talk to her about. How strange that they both had the same one. Tilly remembered the funny look and the pale colour he'd turned when she'd explained how she'd been adopted. What was going on?

As she waited, Tilly ran her hands through Solo's mane and tail, which he seemed to enjoy. She gathered the loose hairs and twisted them together.

"I'll make him a bracelet of *your* tail hairs," she whispered. "Since you're such a wonderful horse!"

Nine

Ten minutes later Brook appeared.
He was holding a large silver trophy
and a red rosette. When he
saw Tilly, he grinned.

"It's thanks to you I
got this," he said. "You
and your detective
work! And you too,
Solo, of course, I could
never have done it
without you!"

85

He turned to Solo, who began nuzzling his shoulder. Brook whispered in his ear and patted him affectionately. It was clear they were the best of friends and it was lovely to see. It reminded Tilly of the special relationships she had with her favourite horses, especially Magic Spirit.

"Rosie and I have been waiting for you," explained Tilly. "You said you wanted to talk."

"Yes. Definitely," Brook answered, with urgency in his voice. "It's really important. What you said about . . ."

But as he was about to explain, a crowd of Cavendish Hall sixth form boys came towards him, shouting his name.

"Brook! Brook! Over here! Show us the trophy! Good one, mate!"

"Uh, cheers," said Brook, not sure where to look.

One of them ruffled his hair.

"Nice one, Brooky Boy!" they grinned. "We knew you'd do it!"

"Let's celebrate. Come and get a snack with us. We're going to the food tent."

"Er, I'll be along in a bit," said Brook.

"Suit yourself."

The boys walked away and Brook turned back to Tilly.

"Sorry about that. They're friends of mine. As I was saying . . ."

"Brook! There you are!" Another voice interrupted them. This time it was a man in a flat cap and grey suit. He was holding a clipboard and looking very efficient. Tilly recognised him as one of the officials.

88

"Hi, Mr Henshall," said Brook.

"Hello there, and hello to . . .?"

Mr Henshall nodded at Tilly. Tilly smiled.

"This is my . . . friend . . . Tilly Redbrow," explained Brook. "And Tilly, this is Mr Henshall. He's the top riding instructor at Cavendish Hall and very high up in the Cosford Pony Club. He taught me everything I know."

Mr Henshall chuckled.

"Not so, young man. It's talent that's got you to where you are. Talent, hard work, and one of the finest horses around. And you, Tilly, I watched you compete in the first class. I always keep my eye on new riders. You showed promise – keep it up! I understand you're having lessons from Angela Fisher at Silver Shoe Farm – she's got a fantastic event record, you could learn a lot from her. Just watch the lower leg position over the fence. Heels down, remember."

Tilly blushed.

"Thanks," she whispered. "I'll work on that."

"Wow, Tilly, Angela Fisher!" said Brook. "She's amazing! I'd love to meet her . . ."

"They want you for a photo call, Brook," said Mr Henshall, interrupting him. "The local press are all here, and rumour has it the Mayor will be putting in an appearance. As soon as you're ready – quick sharp."

"Okay," said Brook. "But I need to talk to Tilly first."

Mr Henshall marched away clutching his clipboard to his chest.

"He seems nice," said Tilly.

"He's all right," said Brook, shrugging. "But listen, what I wanted to talk to you about is . . ."

"There they are!"

This time, it was Tilly interrupting the conversation.

"Who?"

"The girls who took your bracelet."

Tilly pointed to a gang of girls, who were hovering nearby, whispering and giggling. It was obvious they were talking about Brook.

"I might have known," he groaned. "They're known as the Ashton-Smith fan club. For some reason they've got it into their heads that I'm their hero. They drive me nuts! Any second now they'll be over here, fussing and following me about. Do you know what I reckon?" he whispered, with a glint in his eye.

"What?"

"We get right away from here. It's the only chance we've got of having a private conversation."

Before Tilly could say anything, Brook was swinging himself on to Solo's back.

"Come on," he said. "Let's go!"

Rosie snorted and nodded her head, as if she was saying, *Please, Tilly, can I come too?* She obviously liked Solo. Without hesitation, Tilly mounted, and together they made their way out of the crowds, towards the open fields.

Ten

Brook, Solo, Rosie and Tilly trotted for five
or so minutes, through the
fields, and into a quiet
wooded area. It was a
beautiful day for hacking
in the countryside, with a
vast blue sky stretching
above them. As they entered
the wood, they climbed off
their horses and walked with
them side by side. They could

hear the distant sound of
the horse show, but it was
so peaceful where they
were. The trees echoed
with the sound of
woodpeckers and song
thrushes, and sunlight
dappled the path beneath
them. Eventually they
came to a small glade.

"I love it here," said
Brook. "I used to come
here riding when I was
younger."

"It's beautiful," said
Tilly.

Brook and Tilly sat
down on a fallen log and
let the horses munch on
the fresh green grass as
they held on to them.

"Show me your
bracelet again," said
Brook.

Tilly held out her wrist and Brook did the same.

"They're an exact match," exclaimed Tilly. "The colour of the hairs, the clasp – everything! I thought mine was unique. Where did you say you bought yours from?"

"That's the thing," said Brook. "I didn't buy it from anywhere. I've had it all my life. Like you, I've always worn it. Even before . . . before I was adopted."

"The same!" gasped Tilly, wide-eyed.

"Well, yes. And that's got me thinking," said Brook thoughtfully. "If, perhaps, there was another child, not just me, who could have been adopted too?"

"I don't know anything," said Tilly. "The only link I've got is this bracelet – and an old photograph."

Brook paused. He seemed puzzled for a moment then he reached into his jacket pocket.

"Like this?" he asked, drawing out a tattered square of paper and passing it to Tilly.

"This is a photo of *my* real mum," he explained. "I carry it everywhere with me."

Tilly stared down at the image and couldn't believe her eyes. She recognised the hair, the face, the Native American outfit and, of course, the Appaloosa horse. The only differences were that the woman was standing side on, and from that angle, she was clearly pregnant; and standing beside her, holding her hand, was another

child, maybe four years old, smiling
through dark curly hair.

At first it was hard to talk. Tilly's
mouth dropped open and her mind did
somersaults.

"T-t-that's her!" she stammered, her
hands trembling. "That's *my* mum!"

Brook leaned in and pointed to the
child in the photograph.

"And that's me, when I was little."

Tilly looked at him. The smile and the
hair had hardly changed.

"And that bump," he said. "I guess,
maybe, that's you? I've always wondered . . ."

"You and me?" Tilly stuttered.

"We've got the same mum – we're
brother and sister!"

"I have very vague memories of it all.
We lived in America at first – that's where
the photograph was taken – but we came to
England just before you were born. Not
long after, my mum – *our* mum – died in a
car crash. There was no other family to look
after us so we were put up for adoption.

I guess that's when we went our separate ways. You with your family, me with mine . . ."

"And now we've found each other," said Tilly, beaming, her eyes brimming with tears. "The horsehair bracelets have brought us back together."

And then they hugged. For a very long time.

Eleven

It was late by the time Tilly and Brook got back to the horse show. The stalls and trophy tables were being packed away. Most of the horses were in their boxes or being prepared for the journey home.

"I need to find Mia," said Tilly. "Her mum is giving me a

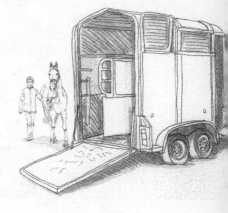

lift home. She'll be wondering where I've been – and Rosie. They'll think I've kidnapped her."

"Horse-napped, you mean!" said Brook. "I suppose I'd better find my people too. No doubt they'll all be panicking. Let's meet up tomorrow – I've got so much to tell you. And, Tilly," he paused and looked into her eyes. "I'm so glad I've found you."

"Me too. Before you go," said Tilly. "I made you this."

She tugged the horsehair bracelet she'd made earlier from her pocket and gave it to Brook.

"I recognise the colour of that hair," said Brook. "It's Solo's!"

"Yes. I made it while I was waiting for you. I make them from the tails of all my favourite horses. I give them to my friends."

"*And* family," Brook said, nodding. "It's lovely, Tilly. I'll always wear it. It will remind me of this day."

"There you are, young man!"

It was Brook's riding instructor, Mr Henshall.

"We've been searching for you. You missed the entire photo call. The Mayor of Seaton was there. He wanted to talk to you!"

He clamped his hands to his head, and gave a frazzled sigh.

Brook gave Tilly a little smile, and then he and Solo were ushered away.

"Wow!" said Tilly, staring at Rosie, dumbfounded by everything that had happened. She clutched her horsehair bracelet and held it close to her heart.

"What a day! My first horse show, and I get second place in my category. And *then* I find out that I've got an older brother, a real, breathing, living brother! And it happens to be Brook, who is the nicest guy in the world!"

Rosie bowed her head and affectionately nibbled Tilly's shoulder.

"Thanks for going through it all with me," said Tilly, stroking Rosie's nose. "Let's go and find Mia."

Mia and her mum were standing by their horse box, talking to some of the other Pony Club mums. As Tilly and Rosie approached they waved.

"Sorry we disappeared," said Tilly. "I had something I needed to . . ."

It was too much to explain in one go.

"I had something to do, that's all."

"That's fine," said Mia. "Cally said she

saw you go off for a ride with Brook
Ashton-Smith. We knew you'd be safe.
But how come you're so pally with him
all of sudden? What's going on?"

"Um," said Tilly, smiling to herself.
"Let's just say it's complicated."

"Tell me!"

"I will . . . soon. I promise."

Together the girls removed Rosie's
saddle, put her travelling gear on, and
arranged her protective clothing. They laid
a sweat rug over her and gave her a drink of
water, to make sure she wasn't dehydrated
after all her activity. Tilly tidied the horse
box and hung a fresh hay-net, then it was
time to load her. Rosie stepped up
obediently. She was probably glad to be
going home, tired after all the adventure.

As they trundled out of the field, Tilly
began to feel tired herself. Everything
seemed to be drifting around her. Mia's
mum switched on the radio and the music
fluttered in and out of her ears. The
countryside rolled by in a blur: fields,

farms, rivers and trees. Mia chattered away, about the different competitions of the day and who she thought had jumped best, but all Tilly could do was nod and smile.

Eventually they pulled up at the Redbrow house. Tilly thanked Mia and her mum for the lift. She peered inside the horse box, blew kisses to Rosie, and went to her front door. Her dad opened it before she had a chance to ring the bell.

"How's my show jumping super star?!" he said, grinning and throwing his arms around her.

"Great, Dad! I feel great!"

"You look as though you've had a busy day. Did anything exciting happen?"

Tilly paused for a moment.

"Er, yeah, you could say that," she smiled, twiddling the strands of her horsehair bracelet. "Where's Mum? Let's sit down and I'll tell you all about it."

As they walked arm-in-arm into the cosiness of the living room, Tilly felt warm and wonderful. She had the Redbrows, who

would always be her number one family.
She had her prize-winning pony, Rosie. She
had Magic, and all of the lovely horses and
people at Silver Shoe Farm. And now she
had Brook.

And it had all started with Magic Spirit. The day she'd found him, abandoned at the roadside, was the day her Silver Shoe Farm adventures had begun. Finding him was what led her to Angela, who led her to Mia and Cally, who had led her, ultimately, although they didn't know it yet, to her long-lost brother.

She thought of Magic now, happily munching grass in the long field, swishing his tail and shaking his mane. He, she realised, was in her destiny. The idea of

this made her feel very, very happy. And the idea of what was going to happen in their future together made her feel even happier. In that instant, she knew they were meant for each other – best of friends, horse and rider, the perfect combination.

Pippa's Top Tips

In preparation for a competition, ensure your pony is looking his best. Use a special plaiting needle and thread to make plaits extra-secure.

Always check that your pony is well-shod. You don't want to be competing with loose shoes.

If you have to travel to your competition, make sure your pony is well-protected with all the correct gear, like travelling boots and a sweat rug.

Don't forget to take water and hay for your pony. They'll be working hard, after all!

Watch professional show jumpers to pick up tips — you'll see they seem barely to move and keep their lower legs completely still.

When you jump, focus on using your legs, rather than driving and pushing with your seat.

The first landing stride after a jump is the first approach stride to the next fence, so focus on looking straight ahead and riding away from the fence.

Don't let nerves get the better of you. However daunting the jumps may seem, it's important to stay calm and focus on your rhythm and balance.

If things go wrong, try to stay positive and learn from your mistakes.

There's no easy route to success – the best riders get where they are through hard work, dedication and practice.

For more about Tilly and Silver Shoe Farm –
including pony tips, quizzes and everything
you ever wanted to know about horses –
visit www.tillysponytails.co.uk